Good-bye, Baby Max

Written by Diane Cantrell

Illustrated by Heather Castles

Bridgeway
Books

Good-bye, Baby Max
Published by Bridgeway Books
P.O. Box 80107
Austin, Texas 78758

For more information about our books, please write to us, call 512.478.2028, or visit our website at www.bridgewaybooks.net.

Library of Congress Control Number: 2007930327

ISBN-13: 978-1-933538-95-2
ISBN-10: 1-933538-95-3

10 9 8 7 6 5 4 3 2 1

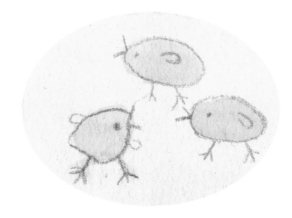

Dedicated to the memory of my father,
John H. Mack, who will always live in my heart.

A Special Thanks To:
Debi Bradshaw for her inspiration
Rich Cantrell for his never-ending support
Paulie Cantrell for his quiet impact on the world

Spring has arrived.
    Birds are building their nests.
And cold winter days
    are now laid to rest.

The children are thrilled,
for soon they will greet
Three baby chicks,
so soft and so sweet.

They wait and they wait
   for the three chicks to hatch.
They're already named...
      Dora, Spiderman, and Max.

One morning, as Leticia takes
her turn at Show and Tell,
The baby chicks struggle
to get out of their shells.

It doesn't take long
   before Dora breaks free,
And Spiderman follows,
   as healthy as can be.

But Max pecks and pecks,
   trying to crack open his shell,
And Mrs. B. worries
   he may not do well.

Chris sees the look
    on his kind teacher's face,
He asks, "Is Max gonna die?"
    as his heart starts to race.

Mrs. B. answers,
    "I think Max must be weak.
After school I'll take him
    to see Dr. McBeak."

The next morning the children
come scurrying in,
Anxious to hear how
baby Max has been.

When all of the children
have finally arrived,
Mrs. B. breaks the news.
Baby Max has died.

Silence falls over the room.
  Liz and Rob begin to cry.
"Don't worry," says Mrs. B.
  "We'll find a way to say good-bye."

"We had a funeral for grandma!" Riley exclaims.
  "Maybe for Max we could do the same?"
Jeremy joins in. "We had a memorial for Uncle Jim.
  People sang songs and told stories about him."
So they plan a funeral to have the next day,
  With songs and prayers and kind words to say.

In the morning they arrive
dressed up in their best,
To show their respect
as they lay Max to rest.

The children quietly march
to the oak tree and stop,
As Mrs. B. carries Max
in a red plastic box.

The children begin to sing,
"Oh, say can you see?"
Before placing the box
under the big old oak tree.

Then it's time for them
    to say their last good-bye,
And Mrs. B. tells them
    not to worry if they cry.

Ramona walks past,
    leaving a picture for baby Max,
And so do Alicia, Hector, and Jack.

They slowly walk back
    to the classroom that day,
Returning to their lessons
    and projects with clay.
As Sarah molds clay
    into letters that spell MAX,
Nathaniel designs
    a memorial plaque.

Cassandra thinks about Max
  and begins weeping,
When all of a sudden
  they hear Spiderman cheeping!

Dora joins in,
   as if singing a song,
Reminding the children
   that life travels on.

The children quietly watch
   the baby chicks play,
Knowing that soon
   they'll have happier days.

The next week at Show and Tell,
Leticia shows off her art,
Reminding them all that Max
lives on in their hearts.

Baby Max, We will love you forever!

 Diane Cantrell is a former kindergarten teacher who presently works as a Licensed Professional Counselor and Life Coach. In her spare time she loves going to movies, dining out, designing hooked rugs, and hanging out with her friends. Diane lives in San Antonio, Texas with her husband, Rich, and their three dogs, Precious, Sunday, and Mr. Lee.

 Heather Castles is a children's book illustrator who likes inchworms, dandelion puffs, and leopard print purses. Heather and her husband, Ben, live in Australia and like to go hiking to spot kangaroos, koalas, and kookaburras.

A Note To Parents and Educators :

In my work as a counselor I have had the privilege of working with a wide range of clients including children, teens, adults, and the geriatric population. I have found that a common thread woven through all stages of one's life is the issue of loss.

Unfortunately, the subject of death and loss is an uncomfortable topic for many adults. Many times we fear that discussing such topics will cause a child to be sad or fearful. Ironically, it is our inability to address these issues that send the message to children that death is to be feared and that feelings of sadness should be avoided at all cost.

This book was written to serve as a springboard for discussion among parents, children, teachers, counselors, and healthcare professionals around this emotionally laden topic. The various rituals that our culture embraces in coping with death are discussed, as are the feelings that emerge during loss. Though the book focuses on loss through death, it hopefully will encourage dialogue around other important losses in one's life and the importance of grieving them as well.